GREAT CAREERS IN THE SPORTS INDUSTRY™

A DREAM JOB AS A SPORTS STATISTICIAN

MARTY GITLIN

Rosen YA™
New York

Published in 2018 by The Rosen Publishing Group, Inc.
29 East 21st Street, New York, NY 10010

First Edition

Library of Congress Cataloging-in-Publication Data

Names: Gitlin, Marty, author.
Title: A Dream Job as a Sports Statistician / Marty Gitlin.
Description: New York : Rosen Publishing, 2018. | Series: Great Careers in the Sports Industry | Includes bibliographical references and index. | Audience: Grades 7–12.
Identifiers: LCCN 2017018430 | ISBN 9781538381380 (library bound) | ISBN 9781508178613 (paperback)
Subjects: LCSH: Sports—Statistics—Juvenile literature. | Statisticians—Juvenile literature. | Sports—Vocational guidance—Juvenile literature.
Classification: LCC GV741 .G58 2018 | DDC 796.023—dc23
LC record available at https://lccn.loc.gov/2017018430

Manufactured in China

CONTENTS

INTRODUCTION

Predicting where top college football players will land in the NFL draft is a difficult task made easier by those with the knowledge and talent to analyze statistics.

It is a cold, snowy March evening. But it's warm in the front office of the local National Football League (NFL) franchise. And the debate is heating up.

The general manager and his staff are discussing the upcoming draft. They all know that their team needs a quarterback. That is where their agreement ends. They cannot decide which college talent to select in the first round.

They pore over statistics. They examine the percentage of passes each candidate completed. They consider the number of touchdowns and interceptions thrown. Yet there is so much more to analyze. They argue over which quarterback boasts the greatest arm strength. They examine how fast each has run the forty-yard dash. They compare numbers that indicate elusiveness and how quickly each prospect releases the ball.

The team must make the right decision. It will pay the chosen quarterback millions of dollars. The fans of their team are depending on them. Folks will not pay to watch a loser. And the quarterback is the most important player on the field. That means every statistic the general manager and his staff studies is critical.

While they debate, one lone statistician is sitting at a long table a few miles down the road. She works for a production company televising a

National Basketball Association (NBA) game. She is busy and alert. She must keep track of a monitor that offers basic player and team statistics.

She notices that the center has made ten of twenty shots, with seven of the ten from fifteen feet (4.6 meters) or less. She shares that tidbit with the television announcers, who inform the viewers. She realizes that the point guard has set a personal record by grabbing seven rebounds in one quarter. That, too, is fodder for the media. She must perform her tasks quickly. She cannot take her eyes off the court or she might miss something important.

On the other side of town sits a fantasy sports analyst. His job today is to break down the statistics of every catcher in Major League Baseball. Millions of people are preparing for their fantasy drafts, and they need his advice.

He is in the process of predicting how many home runs a particular player will hit that season. He asks himself questions based on statistics. Has his home run total been increasing in recent years? Is the ballpark he plays in conducive to home run hitters? Will he face strong or weak pitching within the division in which his team plays? Should he be selected in the first round of upcoming drafts? His advice could make or break a season for fantasy owners.

Sports and statistics have been linked since the nineteenth century. However, statistics have never been more important to all who are involved in sports than they are today. Jobs that combine the two can be fun and fulfilling. Opportunities have been growing in this industry for those with talent and passion. Preparing for such a career requires knowledge about the myriad of sports jobs and how they relate to statistics.

Chapter 1

A TREE WITH MANY BRANCHES

Some compile statistics. Others analyze statistics. Still others utilize statistics. One and all perform tasks critical to the world of sports. But only those who keep statistics during games and provide them for others can truly be called statisticians.

Statisticians can be employed by many different outlets. They often work for production companies responsible for televising sporting events. They sometimes toil for teams. The major American and Canadian franchises that utilize statisticians include the NFL, Canadian Football League (CFL), National Basketball Association (NBA), National Hockey League (NHL), and Major League Soccer (MLS). Major league baseball teams hire in-game scorekeepers, as well as experts in a new wave of statistical study called analytics.

Teams in the NFL, NBA, and NHL boast official stat crews who track every play, as well as individual and team statistics. They then produce summaries for

Statisticians covering games in the NHL and in other professional sports leagues must have an eye for the trends of individual players and teams.

the media to use in their reports and their respective leagues to determine leaders in various statistical categories. The stat crews update basic numbers during games, which allows statisticians working with radio and television announcers to detect and pass along trends in team and player performance. They also update statistics on a daily basis throughout the season to help prepare the media for upcoming games.

Many other statisticians work as free agents who can pitch their talents and experience to keep themselves busy all year. Among these is Tom Bochenek, who serves as a game-day statistician for production crews that cover the MLB Cleveland Indians and NBA Cleveland Cavaliers, as well as college basketball and college football. Bochenek is also the head statistician of the Cleveland Browns. He has extensive knowledge of all major sports, which proves critical to his career. It allows him to find employment as a statistician every season. Bochenek explains:

> I am not paid by the Indians or Cavaliers, only through the production companies that hire me. I am the only stats person for the Indians and Cavaliers games. I work with the TV announcers. No matter who I work

The announcers at this college basketball game depend on statisticians to provide interesting information they can pass on to their television viewers.

> for, my task is to provide objective details of what is happening for each game.
>
> If the Cavaliers or Indians are not playing well, it is my duty to report the stats that back up why they are losing as much as when they are winning. I do intense pre-game work on trends, compile detailed information, and then provide that data to the announcers. I arrive at the ballpark and arena much earlier than anyone so I can do research. There is plenty of communication that goes on between the announcers and me.

The most pressing in-game task of those employed by production companies is to gather numbers from the action on the field, court, or ice. They keep track of every player and team statistic imaginable. They understand which stats are of interest. Their job is to provide trends for broadcasters, who then relay the noteworthy tidbits immediately to their listeners. Organizations that hire statisticians are most interested in experienced talents who can detect tendencies in the performance of athletes and teams.

GOING STAT-CRAZY

The need for more intricate statistics has grown in recent years. The media, fans, and front offices do not simply want to know the basic numbers, such as batting averages or goals scored. They seek detailed trends. They might want to learn the shooting percentage of a basketball player when well covered by a defender over the past month; the strikeouts a pitcher has completed with his curveball, as opposed to his fastball, against left-handed hitters; or the average yards-per-catch of a wide receiver against the zone defense, as opposed to a man-to-man defense.

Such stats help explain not just how an athlete is performing, but why he or she is succeeding or failing. Statisticians who can prove they can provide more detailed information are more likely to be hired. Teams are particularly focused on finding statisticians who can provide exhaustive research. After all, they must make personnel decisions based on statistics. They pay players millions of dollars to perform. They will only pay statisticians with the knowledge and the ability to deliver numbers and trends that will help them make the most difficult choices.

Among those who understand the business is Keith Woolner. He worked for nearly a decade as Director of Research and Development for *Baseball Prospectus*, a publication that provides statistical analysis of the sport. He has toiled for more than a decade since landing in the front office of the Cleveland Indians. Woolner claims that the need for statisticians should continue to grow. And not only in the realm of player analysis. Woolner

Sports fans appreciate statistical data and analysis that increase their knowledge and allow them to discuss their favorite athletes and teams more intelligently.

told the American Statistical Association:

> I think there will be an increasing demand for statisticians who both understand their sport's unique characteristics and can identify the right statistical methods to apply to a problem. More and more, teams are even looking beyond their sports operations department and employing statistical techniques on their ticketing, marketing, ballpark or stadium operations, personnel scheduling, food and beverage, and merchan-

THE SPECIAL TASK OF THE BASEBALL SCOREKEEPER

Every team in the NBA and NFL has its own stat crew. Those in the MLB do not. However, the league does hire a very important statistician for every team. He or she is the official scorer.

The official scorer tracks every play in all eighty-one home games during the regular season and more if the team qualifies for the playoffs. He or she uses the sport's codes to signify what happened on each play. Every position on the field is numbered. For instance, the scorekeeper would mark a fly ball caught by the center fielder as "F-8" or a groundout fielded by the shortstop and thrown to the first baseman as "6-3."

But the official scorekeeper has a more controversial job to perform. He or she must decide whether a fielder is charged with an error or if the batter is credited with a base hit on a particular play. It is his or her judgment alone—and these rulings sometimes anger the players in question. Scoring rules state that an error must be charged when a play is not made that should be completed with reasonable effort.

Players and managers have been known to criticize official scorers for their judgment. Their calls on hits and errors even affect pitchers' statistics. Runs scored against them often do not raise their earned run average when the runner that crosses home plate reaches base or scores due to an error.

dising data. There are many ways an analyst could help a club in those areas.

Major League Baseball (MLB) jumped ahead of its sports counterparts in embracing more advanced stats. That means some MLB franchises might already be stocked with statisticians who can offer in-depth data. But others are still adding statisticians to their front offices and could be for quite some time.

Meanwhile, teams in the other major sports are still studying the benefits of employing those well-versed in providing more detailed statistics. They are learning that such statistics can be analyzed and utilized to best serve their organizations. Habits are hard to break. Some teams remain stuck in the statistics stone age. But many of those in all sports have embraced the new wave of analysis and have hired statisticians who can deliver usable research.

THE NEED FOR ANALYSTS

Sport teams need more than just statisticians. A growing number of jobs have become available in many different areas of sports for people who are adept with statistics. Those who can go beyond gathering numbers and analyze them for the benefit of teams, media outlets, and fans could land higher-paying jobs. But few statisticians are hired out of college. They must first gain experience.

Professional sports teams hire dozens of employees who study and utilize statistical information. Among them are scouts, who examine stats before and after watching high school, college, or professional athletes. They then compile their own analysis based on observation and report to those who make personnel decisions for their organizations. The in-depth numbers that show the potential of athletes play a huge role in determining which players teams acquire through the draft, trades, or free agency.

Fans of those teams also benefit from the work of statisticians. Numbers alone fuel discussion and debate. Few diversions lend themselves more to statistics than

The joy of watching sports is heightened by statistical information. The sharp analysts who keep track of individual and team trends provide these statistics to the announcers.

sports. Millions of fans pore over the numbers compiled by statisticians to form opinions on athletes and teams. They use that knowledge to express themselves intelligently about sports. Statistics often serve as ammunition to make points when conversations about sports become a bit heated.

Since the turn of the century, fans have been able to cite statistics to express their views on sports on the growing number of social media sites. Statistics strengthen their feelings as they express their assertions on comment sections of sports websites or on highly popular social media outlets such as Facebook and Twitter. Statistics are usually the basis for most points made about an athlete or team.

Fans have grown far more sophisticated in their understanding and use of statistical analysis as researchers have provided greater depth in their studies. A fan might argue that one baseball player boasts more power than another because his home run left the bat traveling 114 miles per hour (183 kilometers per hour). Another could claim that a college running back should be drafted in the first round because it took him just 1.8 seconds to break through a hole along the line. Such intricate numbers had not been produced by statisticians until recent years. And they promise to grow more advanced in the future.

Though teams and fans benefit greatly from the work of statisticians, one could argue that the media profits the most. Sportscasters and sportswriters greatly depend upon statisticians to provide information that can be imparted to radio listeners, television viewers, and readers.

But statisticians do not just aid the media as the action on the floor, field, or ice unfolds. They help them do their jobs before and after games as well. The numbers they compile allow sportscasters and sportswriters to prepare for their in-game assignments. Statistics give media members a strong idea of what to expect from players and teams. They provide insight into matchups between players.

For instance, a baseball writer might learn through statistics that a weak hitter has a .500 batting average against an all-star pitcher. The writer would then impart that information to his of her readers before the game to explain why the manager placed that hitter in the lineup that night. And he or she would stress that same stat when reporting that the hitter slugged two home runs against the same pitcher.

Statisticians are indeed invaluable to sports organizations, fans, and the media. Talented and passionate statisticians are coveted by those who hire them. That is why building experience early in life is so important for a career as a sports statistician.

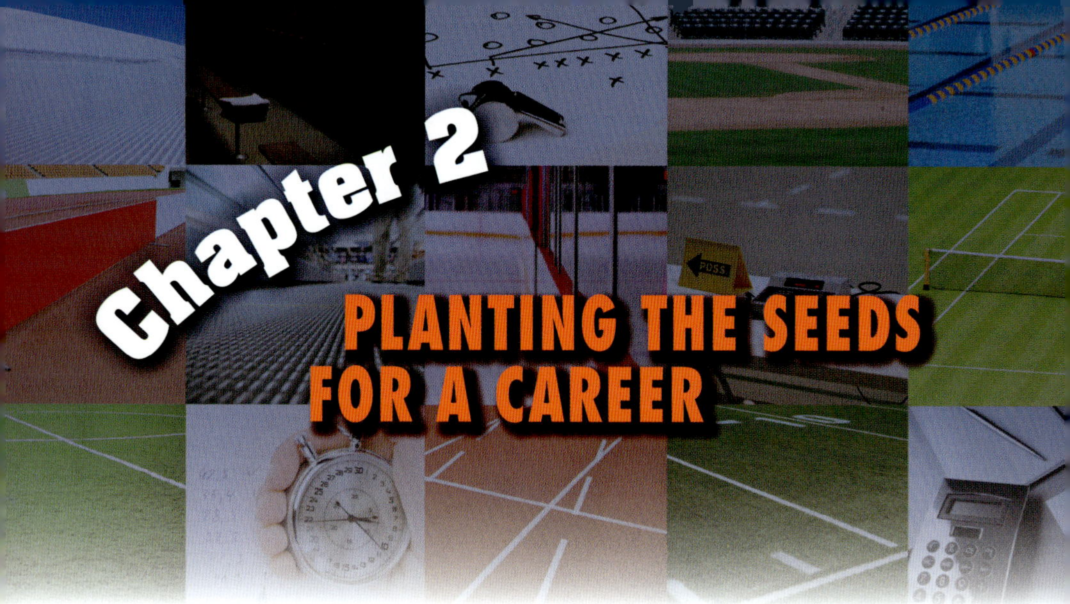

Chapter 2 PLANTING THE SEEDS FOR A CAREER

You have been looking forward to this night all week. Your favorite NBA team is about to embark on what you hope is a run to the championship. The playoffs are set to start.

The original plan was to sit back on your favorite recliner and simply watch the game, but you begin to feel another motivation. You have been thinking about your passion for statistics and sports. And what better way to combine them than by forging a career as a sports statistician. You resolve to take a step toward your goal and create a statistical analysis as you watch the game. You understand that it will not detract from your enjoyment. It will enhance it.

Your work begins an hour before tipoff. You decide to focus on a key matchup between star players on opposing teams. You perform statistical research based on previous clashes between the two to learn who has performed better and why. You study the strengths and weaknesses of both players offensively and defensively. You know that the individual battle will play a huge role in determining which team will win.

The game begins and you are in statistical heaven. You mark down each point, rebound, and assist made by both players. You note every basket scored when one of them is being guarded by the other. You create a chart that shows where on the court both players made and missed their shots. You examine the statistics when the game ends and realize that, indeed, the team boasting the player who won the individual battle also emerged victorious from the game.

You share your information with friends at school the next day. They are impressed. You are proud of yourself because you could have watched the game mindlessly, but instead you went above and beyond to keep detailed statistics—just like the professionals. It leaves you wanting to do more.

Students interested in pursuing a career in sports statistics should not allow opportunities to pass them by. You can ask the athletic director or coach if he or she needs a statistician for a school team that plays your favorite sport. Keeping stats during sporting events and compiling them between games can prove valuable to players, coaches, and fans.

This is one way to watch a game—a better way for those seeking a career as a statistician is to quietly and accurately create your own statistical analysis.

BE A SUPER SPORTS SLEUTH

Ideally, you will expand horizons. Perhaps you are most passionate about baseball, but serving as a statistician for the football and basketball teams as well increases your knowledge of those sports and your chances of landing a job as a statistician later in life. The more you know and experience, the better your opportunity to fulfill your ambitions.

Mike Peticca understands that as well as anyone. He has enjoyed working with statistics for decades. That passion paid off when he landed a job as a statistician for a production company that broadcasts games played by the Cavaliers. He believes that students should take a creative mind-set into

Breaking down and analyzing sports statistics as a student is a fine way to hone one's skills for a future career.

their statistical endeavors. Peticca says:

> If a student would like to be an in-game statistician, certainly it doesn't hurt to develop his or her own system for keeping stats at a game or even while watching on TV. It's very different from when I started 40 years ago. Most of the box score stats are on monitors right in front of you. The announcers you're working for can see the monitors as well. So, you have to be a little more creative and work a little harder at it.
>
> You look for trends. For instance, the monitor might tell you that a player has made 12 of 25 shots. But the screen won't tell you that he's missed 10 of his last 11. Or that a team has

scored no points in its last eight possessions with three turnovers. You would want to tell the announcers that. You can figure things out in your head or by using a small calculator.

Students seeking a career in sports statistics should start with the basics. Learning simply how to keep score of a game is a positive step forward. So is becoming familiar with common statistics in a variety of sports. Those who know little about hockey, for instance, would be wise to watch the sport on television and read box scores in newspapers or online.

Gaining familiarity with many sports does not only broaden horizons, it also opens up the possibility that you will become a fan of another sport. And it adds to the number of sports in which you can become a proficient statistician. Homework and other activities might prevent students from working for several junior high or high school sports teams. But the more experience you gain compiling stats for multiple teams, the better prepared you become to take your career to the next level.

WHEN *NOT* TO ROOT, ROOT, ROOT FOR THE HOME TEAM

As someone who complies statistics for a wide range of sports, Tom Bochenek is a prime example. He understands the benefits of becoming well-rounded in his field.

GET THAT HOMEWORK DONE EARLY

So you want to keep stats during a baseball or football game on television to hone your skills? Better get your homework done early because you're going to be tracking numbers from your couch or easy chair for a while.

NFL and MLB games are much longer than they were in generations past. Fans and league officials have complained about the length of games for years, but the

Students can only make time for sports statistics when the rest of their homework has been completed, though math ties the two together quite well.

issues that caused the problem have proved difficult to solve. Among them is added commercial time between innings of baseball games or time-outs on the gridiron. But advertisers pay big money to the networks, who pay big money to leagues and teams. Cutting down commercial time has been an unpalatable choice to those who profit from them.

The average baseball game has extended past three hours, which is about a half-hour longer than it was in the 1970s. One problem is that pitchers take too long between pitches and hitters often step out of the batter's box. The pace of the game has slowed considerably. NFL contests averaged under two hours and fifty minutes in the 1970s, but have run at least fifteen minutes longer since the turn of the century.

Both leagues allow teams to challenge rulings on the field, which results in delays while officials check replays to make sure they got their calls right. That, too, has served to lengthen games. Attempts to shorten games through a variety of means have proven ineffective.

But he also knows that students should begin with the fundamentals. They must be patient and try to strip away rooting interests. Bochenek says:

> Be disciplined in watching a game and staying with it because games last 3–5 hours. Start with the basics and build up your confidence. This is

> a task in which you can't become involved while showing a rooting interest for a team. That can easily make you lose focus. Stay with the basics of how to score a baseball or basketball game.
>
> Eventually, if you desire to do this, you will seek to become more creative and innovative. When you watch games on TV, pay attention to the information coming from announcers and graphics because they are coming from people compiling the numbers for a purpose. And seek to be great, not just mediocre.

Becoming great takes time. But it is easier to be at least proficient keeping stats for junior high or high school sports, which require less detailed statistics. A high school football statistician might keep individual and team passing, rushing, and receiving yardage. A counterpart maintaining baseball stats would likely keep track of a hitter's batting average, home runs, and runs scored.

Coaches and players appreciate aspiring statisticians with the drive to eventually go beyond what is required. Statisticians who not only track numbers but analyze them as well, provide players and coaches with valuable information. Those who evaluate numbers can cite strengths and weaknesses of players and teams. Students driven to examine statistics and tendencies of opponents help coaches create strategies to

Statistician Harry Robinson is seen here with Kansas State head basketball coach Frank Martin during a game in 2010. Statisticians often help coaches game plan.

combat them in upcoming games.

You should be encouraged to take the next steps beyond basic score keeping and statistics. Gathering information through statistical analysis serves as a wonderful learning experience even if it is never used. But students would prefer their work to be considered worthy. They would like their studies to be used by players and coaches.

This is why it is important to be bold. Social skills are helpful at this point. Those who believe their work can serve as a scouting report of opponents or help their teams improve should not be shy. They should share their information with a coach.

They must convince him or her that their analysis will be helpful.

Even coaches who reject the findings of a statistical report will appreciate the effort. And his or her feedback will help the student prepare a more useful statistical study in the future. Simply gaining the experience and summoning the courage to share findings with a coach can further career ambitions.

"Don't neglect the soft skills," Woolner stresses. "Being successful in sports analysis is not just about having the most data … Many brilliant analysts have struggled because they couldn't get others to listen to and buy into their ideas. It's not enough to be right; you also have to be persuasive. Communication skills, both spoken and written, are important."

So is learning about the myriad job options available to budding statisticians. But it is also critical to understand trends in sports statistics. The most significant is analytics. It has become obvious in recent years that only those who can ride that new wave can succeed as player evaluators in the future. What is most encouraging, however, is that many new opportunities are opening in all sports for those who become adept at analytics.

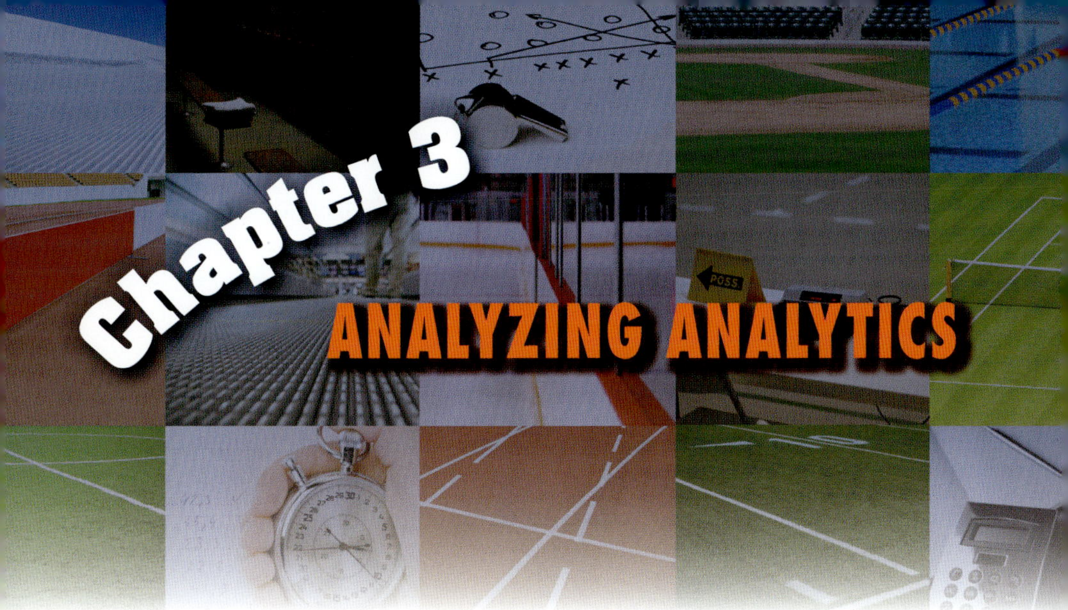

Chapter 3 ANALYZING ANALYTICS

It was the fall of 2011. The MLB playoffs were soon to begin. Interest in the sport was peaking. And folks were flocking to the theaters to watch a film titled *Moneyball.*

The movie told the story of the 2002 Oakland Athletics. Its front office had adopted a revolutionary approach to analyzing and selecting players to fill out its roster, which had first been used by the powerful Indians teams of the late 1990s. The Athletics did not have much money to spend. They could not sign stars to lucrative contracts. They instead rejected long-accepted methods of evaluation, such as scouting, and embraced new theories based on more in-depth statistics to assess talent.

Actor Brad Pitt (*left*) plays the role of Oakland Athletics general manager Billy Beane in the film *Moneyball*, which dramatized the analytics revolution in major league baseball.

Their results were spectacular. The Athletics won 103 games, despite what many believed to be an average roster. They did not create previously unknown statistics. They simply perceived the real value of the old ones. General Manager Billy Beane downplayed the importance of basic stats, such as batting average, in favor of others rarely considered at the time. His philosophy was called sabermetrics and it eventually become known as analytics.

One statistic Beane valued was on-base percentage, which rewards players who reach base via walks as well as hits. Another was slugging percentage. That is calculated through total bases di-

THE REAL MONEYBALL STORY

Most movies stretch the truth a bit to make it more interesting. Moneyball was no exception. The film left the impression that the 2002 Oakland Athletics launched sabermetrics as a new method of evaluating players. But it was the Cleveland Indians in the 1990s that first embraced that approach.

The film features a character named Peter Brand, who works for the Indians before Athletics general manager Billy Beane lures him to Oakland to become the assistant general manager. The Brand character, however, is based on Paul DePodesta, who spent three years with Cleveland before joining Oakland in 1999.

DePodesta later landed his first general manager job with the Los Angeles Dodgers in 2004 before working with the San Diego Padres and the New York Mets. His career took an abrupt turn in 2016 when the struggling NFL Cleveland Browns hired him to serve as their general manager. They hoped that analytics could be translated from the baseball field to the gridiron.

vided by at-bats. For instance, a player who hits a double in four at-bats has a slugging percentage of .500. Sabermetrics revolves around run creation. It measures the ability of hitters to create runs in a variety of ways.

The Athletics proved to be wildly successful during that era. They averaged nearly ninety-four wins per season from 1999 through 2006, despite a payroll

Athletics general manager Billy Beane used analytics to help his team reach the playoffs in 2002 despite a lack of hitting talent.

consistently near the bottom of usual MLB rates. Their hitters ranked near the top of the league in walks and bottom in strikeouts. The Athletics often shunned the work of scouts in favor of sabermetrics when drafting and trading for players. They signed talent rejected by other teams to cheap contracts. Beane valued athletes who could deliver statistics that were undervalued at the time.

His success motivated other teams to embrace sabermetrics. This new trend in statistical study has not eliminated the need for scouts. Scout analyses are based not on statistics, but rather on years of experience watching players perform. Sabermetrics, however, often clashes with scouting. Teams must decide whether to believe their scouts or sabermetrics when evaluating a predicted outcome.

A MATTER OF INTERPRETATION

Some define sabermetrics and analytics differently. They claim that sabermetrics are related solely to statistics and that analytics also take into consideration other data to predict the future success or failure of an athlete.

An NFL general manager might consider the speed at which a quarterback releases a ball or how many seconds it takes a wide receiver to break off into his route. An NBA counterpart could consider numbers that indicate the defensive success of centers

Bloomsburg University quarterback Mike Wagner was not a big name, but his skills and potential could have been analyzed in detail through the science of analytics.

under six-foot-eight-inches tall. An analytics expert in baseball would note exit velocity, which is the miles per hour a baseball travels off the bat of a certain player. One in hockey might even consider the weight that a prospective athlete can bench press. There are few limits to the possible data that can be researched in sports analytics.

Some have debated the potential benefits of analytics in sports aside from baseball. Teams in the NFL, NBA, and NHL have been slower to ride the new wave. They are still trying to figure out the best way to use analytics in predicting an athlete's level of performance. Peticca believes the explanation for that lies within the sports themselves. He also notes that the differences affect job opportunities for prospective statisticians. Peticca says:

> It's pretty obvious that there's a growing reliance on statistical analysis in the NBA, NFL, and Major League Baseball. The issue is analytics versus traditional statistics. Baseball is furthest along in using analytics, so maybe that sport provides the smallest opportunity in the sense there's less new ground to till.

Things that can happen on a basketball court or football field are a little more random than on a

THE GRANDFATHER OF ANALYTICS

No one person is more responsible for the birth of sports analytics than Bill James. Yet James is not a statistician. He is among the most prominent baseball authors and analysts, who proved to be a pioneer in the field of sabermetrics, a term he coined himself.

The Kansas native began authoring The Bill James Baseball Abstract *in the 1970s. His criticism of*

Sportswriter Bill James is considered the founder of baseball analytics, though he did not know he was creating a revolution in sports statistics.

players angered many during the 1980s, but his opinions brought respect from many in the baseball community. Teams and players even went to him to help settle salary disputes because of his knowledge.

James continued to further the cause of sabermetrics and even created new analytical baseball statistics such as runs created. His talents motivated the Florida Marlins to hire him as a full-time statistical analyst in 2002.

He eventually landed a position as Senior Advisor of Baseball Operations for the Boston Red Sox, although he continued to produce books that promoted new sabermetrics and used them to evaluate major league talent. Many believe he will eventually be voted into the Baseball Hall of Fame.

baseball field. Think of what a running back does reversing field compared to an outfielder chasing a fly ball. There's more room for creativity and unpredictability in what the running back is doing. There is therefore more chance for creative thinking and research in football and basketball than there is in baseball.

Indeed, teams in sports aside from baseball have debated how best to make analytics work for them. Their conclusions remain to be seen, but more opportunities await young statisticians who prove they can help teams through analytics.

But learning all about analytics is not the first step. One should become proficient in math to more easily grasp in-depth statistical analysis and how to use it. Students seeking a career in analytics must succeed in algebra. Statistics and probability are two specific subjects that should then be mastered as well.

Another essential is gaining detailed knowledge of a variety of sports. Casual fans with only rooting interests in specific teams are not prepared for a career in sports analytics. A greater familiarity can be gained by playing a sport. But it can also be achieved through an understanding of its rules and strategies.

WATCH, READ, AND LISTEN

You can learn the details of a sport's rules and strategies in a variety of ways: watching sporting events on television, reading about game strategies online and in newspapers, and finding quotes from general managers about how analytics affect player evaluation in drafting, signing free agents, or making trades.

Prospective statisticians can also study in-depth numbers related to athletes. They should become familiar with statistics that analytics experts examine. Which college wide receiver ran the quickest forty-yard dash for NFL scouts? How did a weak weight-lifting session motivate pro basketball teams to pass on a highly rated power forward in the draft? Which NHL player recorded the fastest slap-shot? What major league baseball pitcher boasts the most sink to his curveball?

Analytics take into account all that can be measured. But students should not attempt to cast a wide net if they hope to convince a junior high or high school coach to utilize their statistical

Washington Redskins quarterbacks Colt McCoy and Robert Griffin III are two athletes whose array of skills have been scrutinized by NFL analytics experts.

analysis. They should instead focus on analyzing the strengths and weaknesses of a player from the school team or upcoming opposing team.

Many football and basketball teams at those levels record every game. If you want to gain experience in analytics, you should ask the video coordinator if you can watch a game. Then focus on a particular athlete. Time with a stopwatch how quickly a quarterback releases the ball or a running back hits a hole. Or write down every spot on the court where a point guard makes and misses his shots. You can chart whatever you feel would pique the interest of the coach. Then share this information with him or her.

You can also learn much about analytics through social media. Twitter is filled with statistical information. Most people involved in sports media tweet statistical analytics news and information about athletes. That is especially true when college athletes showcase themselves before annual drafts. The NFL combine in March attracts the premier college football players. They are timed and tested in such skills as sprints, vertical jumps, weight lifting, and quickness drills. Prospective statisticians should pay close attention to such events. They are a hotbed of analytics.

Some believe that the media and even many teams have overrated analytics. They claim that player evaluation can become muddled with too much in-depth statistical information. They contend that some data used by analytics experts is simply not as important as basic stats. Among the critics is Bochenek. He believes that one popular baseball sabermetric statistic known as OPS, which combines on-base and slugging percentage, is useless.

"I have no respect for this type of information," Bochenek says. "And I don't use it at all. I don't respect the networks that use this to death. OPS has no value. It's not right to try to combine two stats like this that has never been done before. There are no standards. I don't refer to these analytic aspects. I feel I can come up with stats and trends that more people will understand. You have to remember who your audience is."

Indeed, what statisticians provide to announcers at games for parroting to viewers might be far less intricate than what analytics experts present to a general manager of a baseball team. In-game statisticians do not require analytics to provide the media with valuable information to impart to audiences. But there seems little doubt that analytics are here to stay and its extensive use will continue to spread from baseball to other major sports.

Students dabbling in sports statistics for the first time should certainly focus on more basic tasks, such as score keeping at school events. But they should also be mindful of the explosion of analytics. And that means evaluating the strengths and weaknesses of athletes through a variety of available information.

Prospective statisticians must provide basic numbers, such as home run and touchdown totals. But it is not too early for them to consider other measurable variables such as speed, quickness, and power of athletes in all sports and at all levels. Gaining knowledge about data used in analytics would prove to be a major step on the road to a career as a sports statistician.

Chapter 4
NOT JUST A FANTASY

The year was 1979. The place was La Rotisserie Française, a French restaurant in New York City. It was then and there that a journalist named Daniel Okrent launched a sports revolution.

Okrent shared a plan with friends whom he had gathered together. He spoke about drafting teams of real major league baseball players before the 1980 season. The statistics those pitchers and hitters produced would translate into point totals for his team and those of his buddies. He believed it would create a fun competition all year long. They all loved the idea. Okrent and his pals then held a draft the following April. Fantasy baseball was born.

The number of fantasy players in the United States alone has grown from that tiny group joining

Daniel Okrent had a fun and creative idea in 1979 that eventually turned millions of sports fans into fantasy players.

Okrent at the eatery to just under fifty-seven million in 2014, according to the Fantasy Sports Trade Association. The same organization predicted that seventy-five million Americans would participate in a fantasy football league in 2015.

New opportunities for folks to immerse themselves in sports statistics professionally has resulted from the skyrocketing popularity of fantasy sports. Fantasy players thirst for athlete analyses that might give them an edge on draft day. They seek advice about players they can add to their rosters during the season. Dozens of websites pay fantasy analysts who study past statistics and predict which players will succeed or fail in the season to come.

Although fantasy football is most popular, millions also participate in fantasy leagues that focus on other sports, including baseball, basketball, hockey, and even golf. Some online sites pay little or nothing for analysts, but some people have made careers out of providing fantasy guidance. They pore over statistics, looking for trends and hints that give them clues about future player performance.

A fantasy football writer might predict that a quarterback will double his touchdown total because his team just added two great wide receivers. A fantasy baseball writer could forecast that a particular shortstop will hit more runs that year because he added

THE LINK TO "WINK" IN FANTASY FOOTBALL

It has been claimed that fantasy sports got their start when a group of baseball enthusiasts gathered in a New York restaurant in 1979. But that is untrue. In fact, it was first conceived seventeen years earlier.

The hero in this story is Bill "Wink" Winkenbach, who was serving as part-owner of the American Football League Oakland Raiders in 1962. His team had

Employees of the 1963 Oakland Raiders, seen here playing against the Buffalo Bills, claim to have given birth to fantasy sports.

lost all five of its games. The season was dreary enough, and one afternoon so was the weather outside. Winkenbach called together a local sportswriter and a Raiders employee to discuss a way to make their lives a bit brighter. He brought up an idea that had been fermenting in his mind for a while. And that was to create their own league based on statistics achieved by actual players on the field.

Winkenbach's buddies devised a scoring system and he did the rest. The Greater Oakland Professional Pigskin Prognosticators League was born. The first draft was held before the 1963 season in the basement of Winkenbach's home. Among the fantasy owners in attendance was a young Raiders scout named Ron Wolf, who later served as a real-life general manager of the Green Bay Packers team that won a Super Bowl.

twenty pounds (9 kg) of muscle. A fantasy basketball writer might point out that an aging center slowed down the previous season and will likely continue to decline the next year.

Those who run fantasy leagues must agree upon a set of rules. Some leagues create schedules in which one fantasy owner competes against another every week. Others feature a free-for-all style in which the standings are determined by point totals at the end of the season. Still others participate in keeper leagues in which athletes remain on the same fantasy teams year after year. Some leagues boast money drafts in which owners bid against each other for real-life players. Others hold straight drafts in which they simply take turns selecting players.

Point distribution also varies from league to league. For instance, one baseball league might limit itself to three batting and three pitching categories that real-life players provide their fantasy owners. The hitting categories might be runs scored, home runs, and runs batted in. The pitching categories could be earned run average, wins, and strikeouts. Other leagues might give one point for a single, two for a double, three for a triple, and four for a home run. Perhaps a pitching win is fifteen points, a save is ten, and a strikeout is one.

A STATISTICAL PLAYGROUND

The skill required to successfully draft a fantasy team in any sport vastly increases knowledge and understanding of a sport and the sport's statistics. Fantasy owners must study the strengths and weaknesses of players at various positions on the field, court, or ice. They must rank each of them to decide which to select for their team. They need to draft with that league's point system in mind. For instance, one football league might award a point for every catch made by a receiver while another only provides points for yardage. That can be the difference between victory and defeat on an NFL Sunday.

Students driven to become fantasy sports analysts can learn a lot by creating their own leagues and determining point systems. But they also gain valuable experience by joining a league that already exists. Predicting the success or failure of real-life players through in-depth analysis is wonderful practice for those seeking careers as statisticians. Those who yearn to maximize the potential of their fantasy teams often delve into research that can be considered analytics.

The statistical analysis required of fantasy owners can prove beneficial to students in their schoolwork, particularly math. They become motivated to work with numbers as they create point systems for their leagues and figure out scoring totals of their teams. Honing such skills helps students make a connection between math in school and in the real world. Students with poor attitudes toward school can even become leaders in math classes as they share their sports knowledge with fellow students.

Fantasy sports provide students a sense of independence and self-empowerment as they contemplate who to draft or trade and decide on lineups every day or week. Participation also tends to bring people together. Families and students often create their own fantasy leagues and compete against each other. Such

Fantasy football owners preparing for fantasy drafts such as this one challenge statistical analysts to provide sage advice about the future performance of NFL players.

bonding experiences can last a lifetime. They can create friendships and bring teenagers closer to their parents.

Understanding the social advantages of fantasy sports can serve as motivation for students considering a career as a statistician. They learn quickly that the most important benefits of participating in a fantasy league are enjoyment and friendly competition. The idea of bringing that joy to others can motivate a student to make statistics his or her life's work. And the rapid growth of fantasy sports seems to ensure there will be a continuing need for statisticians who can evaluate athletes from a fantasy perspective.

The job is not easy. It requires depth of knowledge. One must remain aware of all aspects of athletes' careers in every sport he or she covers to provide sage advice. Fantasy analysts in both the written and electronic media must follow their statistical trends.

AN ANSWER TO EVERY QUESTION

Every stat is attached to questions and answers. For instance, perhaps the touchdown total of a quarterback decreased the previous season. A fantasy analyst must decide why. Did age creep up on the quarterback? Did he receive poor protection from the offensive line? Did the team have terrible running backs, allowing defenses to concentrate on the passing

Fantasy players such as this one can check their statistics anytime and anywhere while making decisions about future lineups based on the advice of fantasy sports analysts.

games? How have those issues been addressed? An expert must answer those questions when advising others on whether or not to select that quarterback in the upcoming fantasy draft.

Fantasy analysts must also keep up with the latest news. Was a pitcher just removed from a game with elbow soreness, thereby casting doubt on his future? Will a basketball player be sidelined for a week to be with his wife, who is about to give birth? Did a coach just tell the media that he has benched his starting running back? Each scenario would require a fantasy owner to alter a lineup to avoid losing valuable points.

Prospective fantasy journalists are never too young to begin thinking like one. And participating in fantasy leagues provides them with that opportunity. One should follow several fantasy experts who abound on Twitter and a myriad of sports-related websites, such as CBSSports.com, ESPN, and Yahoo! Sports. Those who play fantasy football should certainly be tuned in before kickoff on NFL Sundays, when news about real-life lineup changes and injuries play a huge role in determining the best fantasy lineups.

Students who do more than simply participate in a fantasy league will learn valuable lessons. Those who run their own leagues feel empowered. They can track sports news and write reports for fellow league members. They can evaluate and rank players in the lead up to draft day. They can make predictions about player performance and share them. Never mind that they actually help others compete against themselves. The most important benefit of becoming deeply involved in fantasy sports is that it helps one prepare for a career.

The same holds true for those on different avenues to a career as a sports statistician. Any practice is good practice. Any knowledge is good knowledge. It all makes you better prepared when you take that big step onto a college campus.

Chapter 5 FORGING A FINE PATH

A fruitful college education for prospective sports statisticians does not actually begin in college. It starts with picking the ideal school to attend and specific career path to pursue. Those who have already decided which road to travel boast an advantage. But it is never too late to start heading in the right direction. Students seeking to work in sports statistics can target three basic areas of study.

One important area of study is journalism. Gaining experience and knowledge in print or electronic media at the college level is a prerequisite to any career as a sports statistician. Those who become involved in covering sports teams have the opportunity to delve deeper into statistical analysis. Journalism and communications are popular majors.

Students who target a career as a sports statistician should be quite specific when deciding on which schools to apply to. Most preferable are colleges boasting strong athletic programs, a daily newspaper featuring a sports section, as well as a radio and television station that covers sports. All of these provide benefits.

There are many advantages for students who attend journalism schools with a variety of options in the major. These students can select between print and electronic sports media, both of which lend themselves to statistical analysis. They can also contact the sports information director about the possibility of serving as an in-game statistician for the athletic department or campus radio or television networks broadcasting games. And many coaches of college sports teams would be quite appreciative of those dedicated enough to take their talents to the next level and provide them with useful analytics information.

Another college major that can prove beneficial is statistics. The math that is required to earn a degree in statistics is most often unrelated to sports. But students who concentrate on such specifics as data collection and probability are better suited to serve as a statistician for college sports teams than those with weaker mathematics backgrounds.

Prospective statistics majors, however, will eventually want to decide whether their interest in sports is strong enough to select a university with a large athletic presence. Those who enjoy working with statistics, but who do not plan on combining that passion with sports as a career, should consider other options.

Becoming involved in the sports media at the college level is one way to forge a wonderful path to a career as a statistician.

Statistics are used in many professional pursuits, including political science, engineering, and economics.

A third possibility as a major is sports administration. Students who yearn to work in the front office of a professional sports franchise are luckier than those of previous generations. Many universities now offer sports administration majors and degrees. Teams in all major sports utilize talent evaluators as scouts and player personnel decision-makers, whose primary job is to study statistical and empirical data and advise others on which athletes to draft or sign.

NASCAR auto racing employees and interns pose for a photo. Internships can be a valuable experience for those seeking careers in any sports-related field.

Students eyeing work in sports administration must realize that the new wave of analytics has motivated professional sports teams to hire more statisticians. Many other front office jobs are realistic targets for college students. Some of them require a strong grasp of statistics, but they do not fall under the category of statistician. It should also be stressed that pro franchises do hire in-game statisticians who provide stats for the media and leagues in which they participate.

A NEW ROAD TO SUCCESS

Those who do yearn to combine their love for statistics with their love of sports should not be discouraged from pursuing their

A CHALLENGE FOR ANALYTICS MAJORS

Syracuse University launched the first sports analytics program in the United States in August 2017. Students previously majoring in sports administration are allowed to switch over. But not just anyone is eligible to gain a degree in sports analytics. Only those boasting a 3.6 grade point average or better are eligible. And to graduate with this degree a student must complete 125 credit hours.

Among the areas of study offered to analytics majors are math, statistics, and computer pro-

The growing field of sports analytics has motivated Syracuse University to launch an analytics program—other colleges seem certain to follow.

gramming. More specifically, students in this program delve into research methodology, organizational theory, management theory, technology, sports economics, database management, finance, and computer programming relevant to sports analytics. The students are urged to apply the principles they learn to issues sports organizations confront.

But the analytics program does not center only on athlete evaluation. It delves into such sports management topics as sales, marketing, sponsorship, and accounting.

One need not attend a school that offers a major in sports analytics to become proficient at it and land work in that area. Though advantages abound in course studies revolving around the subject, students can still hone their skills through involvement with the media and college sports teams. Researching trends and tendencies of athletes on those teams and on those opposing, not only helps them prepare for upcoming games but can also be used to bolster a résumé and eventually find work in the field.

A more obvious need for college students is a thorough knowledge of individual sports. Though it is ideal to understand the intricacies of all major sports to maximize professional possibilities, those with a desire to work in one particular sport must become experts. Woolner understands this well. He offered his advice to new sports analytics professionals, but his words can be applied to college students as well. Woolner says:

> *Truly understanding the sport you want to analyze professionally is critical to being successful. Knowing the rules of the game; studying how front offices*

operate; finding out how players are recruited, developed, and evaluated; and even just learning the jargon used within the industry will help you ... You'll come to understand what problems are important to the [general manager] and other decision-makers, as well as what information is available, how it's collected, what it means, and what its limitations are.

Also, I recommend keeping up with the discussions in your sport's analytic community so you know about the latest developments and what's considered state of the art in the public sphere. One of the great things about being a sports statistician is getting to follow your favorite websites and blogs as a legitimate part of your job!

Woolner cites that level of domain knowledge as one of three skills sets necessary to become a successful sports statistician. Another is mastering mathematical and statistical techniques that allow students to grasp data. That can be learned through a variety of courses found in applied statistics programs at the college level. Among those talents are designing charts and graphs that help statisticians present and communicate the outcomes of their research.

A third skill is more technical. Woolner believes that understanding and utilizing a variety of statistical software and programming systems is important for those involved in sports statistics, as is reading and interpreting information found in a database. One tool used in sports analytics is SQL, a domain-specific language that helps sort through data and find patterns in an athlete's performance.

dreams. Yet another possible career path has recently arisen. Syracuse University now offers a degree in sports analytics. Other schools seem destined to follow. Since analytics remains the wave of the future in professional sports, those who pursue such a major can forge an easier path to a career in the sports media or as a valuable franchise employee.

IT'S ALL ABOUT TIMING

Deciding which avenue to take toward a career in statistics should ideally be done before you step onto a university campus. One should weigh the advantages and disadvantages of majoring in statistics, sports administration, or journalism while in high school. But prospective sports statisticians can gain a grasp of the specific work they prefer at the college level. And they can base their decision on their experiences.

Those who would rather avoid the more technical and analytical aspects of the business are better served as in-game statisticians who can be employed either by the media or sports franchises. Working college events for a local radio or television station or the athletic department tests these abilities in a more hectic environment than sitting at one's computer analyzing and predicting the performance of a particular athlete.

Peticca is well-aware of the differences. He must capitalize on every opportunity to share pertinent

UCLA is one of hundreds of American universities that feature major sports programs and a pathway to success for prospective sports statisticians.

statistical information with the basketball announcers, who in turn inform their viewers or listeners. Bochenek does the same while working for the Browns. Any play on the field or court might result in an important statistical update. Peticca says:

> Working as a statistician during games is generally very different than working in analytics. To be a good in-game statistician you must be able to quickly record multiple plays as they

happen and be able to recall plays and moments throughout the game. You must be able to recognize key trends, looking at things from team and individual player standpoints. You have to know what the announcers want and what the people doing graphics in the production truck want. You have to keep your cool if there's a surprise request.

In basketball, where things move along at such a rapid pace, it's cool to note something like a team has made 11 shots in a row from outside the paint or that a team has registered an assist on each of its last 16 baskets. Most analytics allows time for research. They don't have the in-the-moment urgency.

College students who serve as in-game statisticians learn that their daily work does not begin nor end during games. They must study statistics that track team and player trends so they can prepare to offer new information when the game action alters those numbers. They must also provide post-game statistics that can prove useful to announcers analyzing the results for viewers and listeners or sportswriters doing the same for readers.

Peticca knows that in-game statisticians working for media outlets can also dabble in analytics on the side. The options are wide open at the college level. Gaining experience in both in-game stats and analytics is critical to making an ideal career decision, as is choosing the right major. Also important is becoming an expert on at least one sport, but preferably more.

Making all the right decisions and developing a strong work ethic should lead to gratifying employment and a fulfilling career. But one must understand that professional franchises, sports production companies, and established media outlets rarely hire statisticians out of college. Understanding where and how to look for work that provides needed experience is critical to success.

Chapter 6
JOBS ANYWHERE AND EVERYWHERE

College is a time for reflection. It is a period when students ask themselves questions about how they will spend the rest of their lives. And their answers often start them on a career path.

Those who wish to become sports statisticians must gain a grasp of what kind of work will bring them happiness and self-fulfillment. They require a knowledge of the job market. Students or recent graduates who gain an understanding of their passion and an awareness of the job openings in the field they choose are on the right road.

But they must also know that professional experience is generally required for statisticians seeking employment. Bochenek highly recommends that graduates ask the sports information director at the school they attended about the possibility of working college games for television or radio production companies. Bochenek states that they are often looking for stat-

These happy graduates have taken a major step forward, but those seeking careers as sports statisticians need more experience.

isticians. Those with backgrounds as statisticians in a variety of sports have the best chance of landing such an assignment.

Statisticians who seek employment in the growing world of sports analytics should be aware that many of the jobs in major league baseball organizations have been filled. And though not all franchises in other major sports have embraced analytics to the point of hiring specialists, the notion has caught on and these fields are considered more viable options for future hires.

Even Instructional League baseball games such as this one can provide young hopefuls a chance to hone their skills as statisticians.

Ben Alomar understands this issue. He toils as an analytics expert for the NBA Oklahoma City Thunder and founded a publication focusing on statistical analysis of sports data titled *Journal of Quantitative Analysis of Sports*. Alomar believes that franchises in sports other than baseball will embrace analytics and hire those who can use the new wave of analysis to maximize their teams' potential.

"There is a natural skepticism of employing any new tool when you have had success previously without it," Alomar says. "As decision-makers gain more exposure to information that analysis can provide, they tend to become more interested."

Those determined to work in baseball should not be discouraged. Every major league baseball franchise boasts at least four minor league affiliates in various areas of the United States that are covered by media outlets. Though the minor league teams do not require analytics experts, the production companies that air their games offer opportunities for statisticians. Those who prove themselves worthy can work their way up the ladder and eventually land jobs with production companies that broadcast major league games.

Many other considerations face young sports statisticians. Among them are time constraints. For instance, a fantasy football writer understands that he or she will be particularly busy leading up to the NFL season, as players prepare for their drafts. And he or she will remain busy throughout the campaign while providing week-to-week advice about lineups, trades, or roster additions.

And those who work a wide variety of sports certainly have difficulty finding time for a relaxing vacation. Just ask Tom Bochenek, who serves as a media statistician covering the Indians, Cavaliers, and college football and basketball and then handles stats as an employee of the Browns. He remains busy all year.

FUTURE JOBS FOR STATISTICIANS

The Bureau of Labor Statistics (BLS) does not specify future job outlooks for sports statisticians, but it does note that employment for statisticians is projected to grow by 34 percent over the next several years—a significantly faster rate than the average for all occupations. The agency foresees the widespread use of statisticians to make more informed business and healthcare decisions, and trends toward analytics indicate a growing need in sports as well. The BLS also cites that statisticians should gain at least a master's degree in statistics or mathematics to land position above entry-level.

The electronic media on campuses can provide opportunities for students and graduates with eyes on statistics careers to become or remain closely involved in sports.

Prospective statisticians enamored with fantasy analysis must take a different tact. The seeds of success can be planted at the college level through work on the campus newspaper, radio station, or television network. All three types of media outlets are available for journalists to hone their skills and specialties. A motivated student who has researched a sport or sports of choice can serve as a fantasy advisor to fellow students and even those in surrounding communities. He or she can be particularly valuable as fantasy drafting time approaches but also throughout sports seasons.

Graduates who yearn to increase their chances of landing jobs as a fantasy analyst must often display their talents for free to smaller online sites. The motivation is to build a résumé and provide writing samples to entities that do pay fantasy analysts, including such well-known websites as ESPN, CBSSports.com, and Yahoo! Sports.

Another option is creating and promoting a fantasy website. You can sell advertising space if it proves popular. Social media outlets such as Facebook and Twitter can make sports fans aware of your site and its fantasy benefits. Even if the site does not prove financially viable, the analysis provided can be used to build a résumé and give paying websites work to consider.

IN A LEAGUE BY THEMSELVES

The immense popularity of college football and basketball has resulted in many conferences that boast their own television networks and broadcast their games. That has opened up opportunities for in-game statisticians, some of whom attended the schools involved in the action on the field. Even individual schools, such as the University of Texas, have launched their own networks.

The Big 10, PAC-12, Atlantic Coast Conference (ACC), and Southeastern Conference (SEC) all feature football, as well as both men's and women's basketball games on their networks. Other sports, such as wrestling, gymnastics, and baseball, are also sometimes shown.

The opportunities for young statisticians could be more pronounced for students or recent graduates of PAC-12 schools. These schools own their own sports networks. The other conferences have teamed up with media giants ESPN and Fox. But the financial success of conference networks in the future could result in more sporting events being televised and more statisticians being hired.

Limiting yourself to fantasy sports is risky. Most work is unpaid, only a comparatively small number of media outlets require fantasy analysts, and neither college athletic departments nor professional teams deal with that aspect of their sports. Far greater opportunities await graduates who are adept and experienced in analytics.

Though few teams outside of baseball have embraced the relatively new science of player evaluation and performance prediction, the number is growing, and it is quite possible that all professional franchises will eventually hire analytics experts. And that is encouraging considering that the five major sports leagues in the United States and Canada house a total of 133 teams.

MLB has taken the lead in hiring analytics experts, but opportunities in that sport still abound. Baseball franchises look beyond player evaluation to

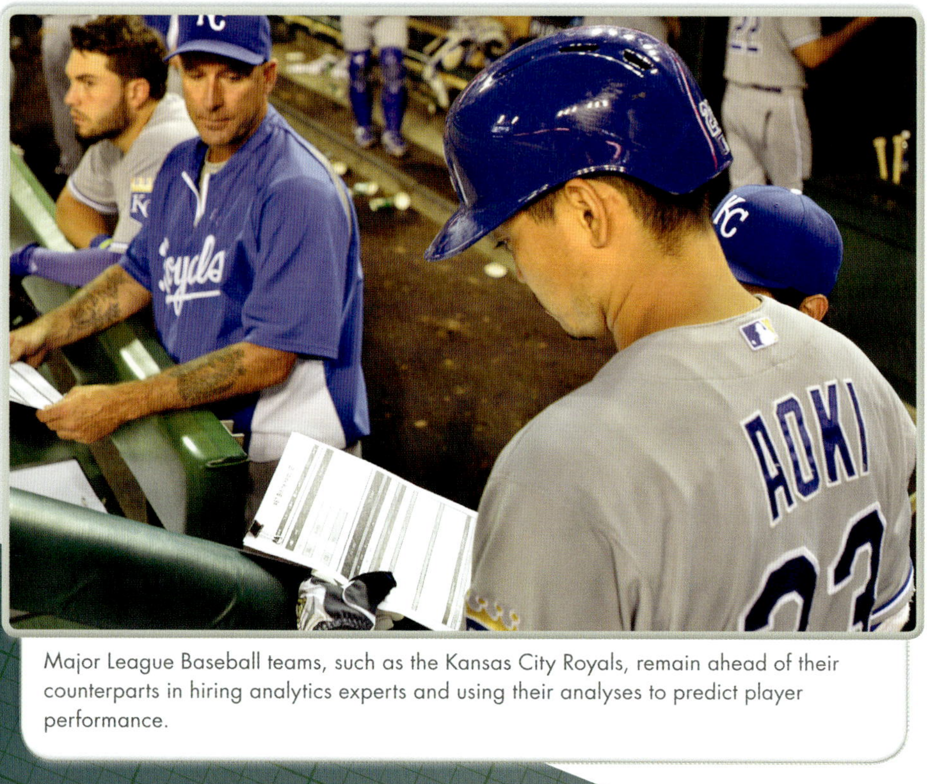

Major League Baseball teams, such as the Kansas City Royals, remain ahead of their counterparts in hiring analytics experts and using their analyses to predict player performance.

all aspects of their operations for research and advice that requires statistical analysts. This is where sports statistics majors with analytics skills can eventually find jobs at the highest levels of sports, even if no openings are available in player evaluation.

OPPORTUNITIES IN SABERMETRICS

An increasing number of online publications have focused on sabermetrics, the in-depth statistical study of baseball players and teams. Among those that pay their personnel are FanGraphs.com and Baseball Prospectus. These websites cater to fantasy owners and hardcore baseball fans while providing information about every player in major league history. They feature analysis and predictions from their writing staffs, as well as podcasts and live chats.

FanGraphs.com breaks down player performance into dozens of categories. Readers can learn the earned run average of a pitcher when the quality of the fielders behind him are removed from the equation. They can find out how consistently hard a batter hits a curveball as opposed to a fastball. They can track the performance of a player in night games in comparison to day games or against right-handed pitchers versus left-handed pitchers.

Baseball particularly lends itself to such intricate statistical study, but the need for more in-depth analysis in the other major sports seems destined to rise. Online opportunities for statisticians who can write about and analyze their sports promise to increase. There is a thirst among a certain segment of sports fans for in-depth information about football, basketball, hockey, and even soccer.

Those yearning to analyze sports statistics should work to take advantages of such prospects. Whether still in college or recently graduated, you must prove you have skills to offer. Collecting and analyzing data about athletes leads to predictions. Showing motivation to complete the process and accuracy in forecasting player and team performance will impress media outlets or teams that want to begin or bolster their analytics staffs. Data can be gathered in many ways, including by serving as an in-game statistician, watching events on television, and finding information online.

Peticca believes that the rooting interest young statisticians might feel for the teams in their hometowns can be parlayed into helpful work experience if they remain objective in their research. The sheer number of players and teams in all major sports can be overwhelming. But focusing on those in one city would provide information craved by the fan base there. Peticca says:

NEW NUMBERS FOR THE NHL

Sports franchises outside of baseball have been more likely to embrace analytics when they have struggled to win than if they have maintained consistent success through traditional player evaluation methods. Those teams have given more hope to analytics specialists who wish to work at the major franchise level.

The perennially poor NFL Cleveland Browns are not the lone example. Another is the NHL Arizona Coyotes, who in 2016 promoted analytics expert John Chayka to their general manager position. At twenty-six-years-old, he became the youngest GM in league history.

Although the NHL has dabbled in more advanced statistical research in recent years, the Coyotes were the first to place their trust in an analytics specialist and place him in such a lofty position in the front office. The trend toward analytics in hockey has been termed "Moneypuck," a play on the name of the movie Moneyball *that brought tremendous attention to sports analytics.*

Hockey teams have used analytics to evaluate talent and gain a competitive edge as they study such statistics as scoring opportunities for and against particular players, the miles-per-hour of a forward's slap shot, or the success of a defenseman clearing the puck out of a zone. Just about any aspect of the sport is fair game.

Desperation, or at least a longing to shake off the doldrums of losing, is most likely to motivate a franchise to turn to analytics. The Browns for instance, have been the worst team in the NFL since 1999. The Coyotes had gone five consecutive years without making the playoffs before promoting Chayka.

I'd think there'd be newspapers and websites that would be interested in someone who can come up with some of his or her own original statistical analysis, especially on the local teams and players. If you're around Chicago, for instance, find ways to break down what

All-star catcher Ivan (Pudge) Rodriguez shakes hands with Dallas Mavericks general manager Donnie Nelson in 2017. Baseball and basketball teams are light years apart in regard to using analytics.

> the Cubs, White Sox, Bulls, Bears, and Blackhawks are doing. Break down individual players. There are so many stats kept these days that the essence of what you do is almost certain to be available somewhere, but find ways to add on that to make it unique and interesting.

Perhaps the most significant and mentally difficult move is changing one's mind-set from that of a fan to general manager. Prospective statisticians, particularly those seeking work in analytics for professional sports teams, must ask themselves what a GM would want to know about a player. Teams are always looking for an edge in player evaluation and development. Gaining an understanding of the analytical insights a general manager craves and providing that information to him or her might make an impression that leads the GM to hire an analyst and build a long-term relationship with the team.

Motivation and talent alone, however, do not ensure employment worthy of those attributes. You must learn how to maximize those skills as you seek work to provide the best chance for success, whether the target is the media or one of the many sports franchises in North America.

Chapter 7 TURNING A DREAM INTO REALITY

The old expression about career success is that "it's not what you know, but who you know." That is quite an exaggeration. Learning a craft and proving one's skills through experience are critical components to landing a desired job.

But there is some truth to it. Relationships alone will not secure work. But cultivating strong business ties through confidence, ability, and kindness win over employers. You must be liked before you can be hired. A budding statistician can gain notoriety for analytical research in sports, but be shunned if he or she is not friendly, humble, and generous with his or her information. Those who hire, want to work only with people who are easy to get along with. That is certainly true about employers that run media outlets, production companies, or player evaluation departments of major sports franchises.

Computer skills are essential for sports statisticians and statistical analysts in the modern era as information can be found and sent online.

Howard Hamilton knows which personal traits are necessary to secure employment in this field. He founded and serves as the Chief Executive Officer of Soccermetrics Research, which seeks to further the use of advanced analytics in the world of soccer. He believes that several intangibles, beyond sheer knowledge and ability, are critical to landing a sought-after job.

"Networking is important, and it's good to be known, but it's even better to be known as someone who does things or writes about interesting things," Hamilton stresses. "Cultivate relationships and be generous with sharing contacts … Be nice and don't be a jerk … Never lose humility. I mean it: Never. Lose. Humility. There is a lot of humility that is lacking in computational endeavors, and especially analytics."

One must also be well-grounded with a practical approach to finding work. Sharing research and outcomes with potential employers is not only generous—it is also smart. Professional sports teams seeking an edge against rivals scour the talent pool to find gifted young analytics researchers. Those who have taken the time and energy to create analytical studies that can be used to predict the performances of professional athletes or aid a franchise in any capacity should send that information to the teams most likely to benefit from them.

But it is also wise not to limit the scope of a job search. A résumé and work samples must be general enough to impress the personnel department of any team in a targeted sport. Prospective analytics specialists should ideally be willing to relocate anywhere in the United States or Canada to gain employment with a professional franchise. Although you might start your job search by looking at the most coveted landing spots, you should recognize that finding a job in sports analytics at this level is very difficult. It certainly might be necessary to maximize the scope of a search to find such a job.

THE QUICKEST ROUTE TO A BASEBALL JOB

Sports analytics expert Nirav Bhardwaj knows all about translating his skills into work with a major league baseball team. He did just that when he landed a job with the Los Angeles Angels. And though he did not remain in the business, he gives sage advice to those who yearn to take the same path.

Bhardwaj believes that a thorough knowledge of the Collective Bargaining Agreement (CBA) between players and owners is a must for anyone who seeks to

The Anaheim Angels might hire analytic experts to study their players, such as outfielders (*left to right*) Ben Revere, Mike Trout, and Kole Calhoun.

find work in baseball operations or player development. One must become an expert on the rules of every transaction, such as trades and free agent signings.

The next step Bhardwaj recommends is to create an analysis report that identifies an issue for a specific team and provides a solution. The work is painstaking, but he claims that a successful report will all but guarantee a front office job. One should understand the issues facing big-spending teams, such as the New York Yankees or Los Angeles Dodgers, and small-market teams, such as the Milwaukee Brewers or Tampa Bay Rays. But it should also be noted that every franchise boasts a different philosophy in regard to player procurement and evaluation. Gaining a knowledge of how each team operates allows one to create a useful analysis report for any one of them.

Major league teams face many issues that can be broken down statistically and debated. Such issues include the successes or failures of long-term contracts in comparison to short-term contracts, signing players to extensions, or taking chances on expensive free agents. The more prospective statisticians have on the history of each team, the better the opportunity to prove they can help.

Bhardwaj also strongly encourages hopeful statistical analysts to pore over articles produced by baseball analytics sites such as FanGraphs.com and Baseball Prospectus. This will help candidates understand which statistics are important and why.

Writing and researching for publications such as FanGraphs.com or *Baseball Prospectus* can be used as a stepping-stone to working with a major-league team. The media provides far fewer opportunities in other major sports for analytics specialists. Statisticians who wish to write about football, basketball, and hockey are greatly limited to fantasy, though future possibilities seem likely to arise given the increased interest in analytics in those sports at the team level.

Bold young statisticians with the knowledge and desire to create opportunities for themselves might take advantage of the lack of online analytics sites focusing on the other sports. For instance, pro football surpassed baseball decades ago as the most popular sport in America. Launching a website that delves deeply into football analytics and works to attract readers could lead to advertising and a money-making venture. If your research gives accurate player evaluations and performance predictions, you could be considered for employment by NFL or CFL teams.

THE ESSENTIAL INTANGIBLES

After all, talent alone does not ensure success. An aggressive mindset, strong résumé, creativity, and impressive work samples all maximize employment

Former president Franklin Roosevelt famously stated that there is nothing to fear but fear itself. That advice should be heeded by those forging a career as a sports statistician.

possibilities. Also important is making contacts in the field with potential employers and established statisticians who can provide career advice. Finding a job can be achieved through networking—asking questions about potential openings and promoting oneself to those already in the business. Letting others know that you are motivated, confident, competent, and helpful can go a long way in achieving your career ambitions.

President Franklin Roosevelt famously proclaimed that there is "nothing to fear but fear itself." That is certainly true for prospective statisticians. You should not be afraid to use social media sites such as LinkedIn to reach out to veterans in the field who can advise you about options for gaining valuable work experience, contacts at production companies, and professional sports franchises that might be willing to take a chance on a young statistician or analytics hopeful.

Social media has indeed increased access to people who can help you jump-start a career. However, the old-fashioned way still has its place. And that is a strong résumé and work samples that show talent and insight. Personal experiences as a statistician should be stressed on a résumé. Those who prove their mettle by attaining a college degree impress potential employers. But prospective candidates who can prove that they will be valuable additions with through previous statistical analysis or in-game experience, will rise above other candidates.

Another important task is to compile a list of references—teams or people who have profited from your work as a statistician. Junior high and high school coaches and athletic directors, university campus media outlets, and sports website editors are essential references. Though professional sports franchises and production companies generally seek out statisticians with vast experience, a college graduate who has experience that extends back a decade or longer certainly boasts an advantage. Adding quotes from references that praise your work ethic and talent can also be helpful.

The final step in landing a job is the interview process. Preparing to speak with an employer can be as important as the conversation itself. You must have a thorough knowledge of the sport about which you are to be interviewed and the needs required of you as a statistician for that particular job before you go into the interview. The team, media outlet, or sports production company is seeking to fill a need. Boasting an appreciation for that need is critical to your success. The importance of putting your best foot forward during the interview cannot be understated. You should speak confidently without bragging and display an engaging personality from the first to the last handshake.

DO YOUR HOMEWORK!

That confidence will not be possible if you have not studied beforehand. You should not merely embark on a cursory examination of the employer, especially if it is a sports franchise or media outlet. Learn about their strengths and weaknesses. If you are being interviewed by a team representative for a job in analytics, find out how deeply that team has delved into analytics previously and with what level of success.

Exploring the struggles a team has experienced can motivate you to cite your successes in that area during the interview. Perhaps your research has revealed that a particular online site is strong in fantasy football, but weak in fantasy basketball. Pointing out your knowledge of fantasy basketball would then be a wise approach, whether in a phone interview or through your résumé and writing samples. One should highlight work that fills the need of an employer.

You should understand that fantasy writers and analytics experts are not statisticians by the strictest definition, but rather statistical analysts. Only those who work for teams or in-game production companies can be defined as statisticians. And, most impor-

Gaining contacts in the field can be a critical component to finding the ideal job, but one must be well-liked as well as talented to maximize potential.

tantly, you should keep in mind that hands-on experience is a prerequisite to gaining employment. Tom Bochenek knows that as well as anyone. He sums up his advice to prospective statisticians:

It's simple. Understand the stats rules, keep your emotions out of the game, show a desire to work at any level of keeping stats, contact the media relations department of the university you attended, and try to find the contact people at the production companies. Try to understand who to contact who can help you get your foot in the door. Many people think they can do stats, but show a creative mind-set and set yourself apart. Establish your credibility with other stats people around the country and create a network with them that will benefit you.

And have fun. Those who enjoy their work are far more likely to find success. Those who love both sports and working with numbers are ideal candidates for careers as sports statisticians. If you are one of them, you must take all the right paths to land a job that best suits your talent and passion.

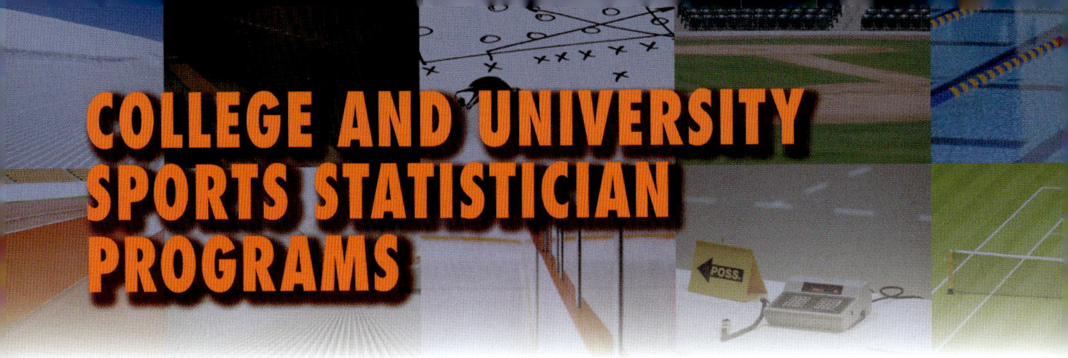

COLLEGE AND UNIVERSITY SPORTS STATISTICIAN PROGRAMS

Eastern Michigan University
Eastern Michigan University Admissions
220 Student Center
Ypsilanti, MI 48197
(734) 487-3060
http://www.emich.edu
Programs of study: sports administration, sports science, media studies and journalism, applied statistics

Indiana University
Indiana University Admissions
300 North Jordan Avenue
Bloomington, IN 47405
(812) 855-0661
https://www.iu.edu
Programs of study: athletic administration, sports management, sports journalism, sports media, statistics

Ohio University
Ohio University Admissions
120 Chubb Hall
Athens, OH 45701
(740) 593-4100
https://www.ohio.edu
Programs of study: athletic administration, sports broadcast and print journalism, mathematical statistics

Seton Hall University
Seton Hall University Admissions
400 South Orange Avenue
South Orange, NJ 07079
(800) 843-4255
https://www.shu.edu
Programs of study: sports management, sports broadcasting, journalism, mathematics, statistics

Syracuse University
Syracuse University
Crouse-Hinds Hall, 900 Crouse Avenue, #100
Syracuse, NY 13244
(315) 443-3611
https://www.syracuse.edu
Programs of study: sports analytics, sports management, broadcast and digital journalism, applied statistics

Temple University
Temple University Admissions
1801 North Broad Street,
Conwell Hall 103
Philadelphia, PA 19122-6096
(888) 340-2222
https://www.temple.edu
Programs of study: sports and recreation management, journalism, statistical science

University of Arkansas
University of Arkansas Admissions
Silas H. Hunt Hall, 471 Garland Avenue
Fayetteville, AK 72701
(479) 575-5346
https://www.uark.edu
Programs of study: recreation and sports management, broadcast journalism, mathematical sciences

University of Connecticut
University of Connecticut Admissions
2131 Hillside Road, #3088
Storrs, CT 06269
(860) 486-3137
http://uconn.edu
Programs of study: sports management, journalism, statistics

University of Florida
University of Florida Admissions
201 Criser Hall
Gainesville, FL 32611-4000
(352) 392-1365
http://www.ufl.edu
Programs of study: sports management, journalism, telecommunications, statistics

University of Massachusetts
University of Massachusetts Admissions
37 Mather Drive
Amherst, MA 01003
(413) 545-0222
http://www.massachusetts.edu
Programs of study: sports management, journalism, mathematics, statistics

University of North Carolina
University of North Carolina Admissions
174 Country Club Road
Chapel Hill, N.C. 27514
(919) 966-3621
http://www.unc.edu
Programs of study: sports science/sports administration, media and journalism, statistics, operations research

University of Ottawa
University of Ottawa Admissions
Tabaret Hall, 75 Laurier Avenue East

Ottawa, ON K1N 6N5, Canada
(877) 868-8292
https://www.uottawa.ca/en
Programs of study: sports management, digital journalism, mathematics, statistics

University of Texas
University of Texas Admissions
110 Inner Campus Drive, Main 13
Austin, TX 78712
(512) 475-7399
http://www.utexas.edu
Programs of study:sports management, sports journalism, statistics, data science

A CAREER AS A SPORTS STATISTICIAN AT A GLANCE

TEAM STATISTICIANS

ACADEMICS

Bachelor's degree, preferably in statistics or mathematics

EXPERIENCE

In-game statistician for junior high school, high school, or college teams

Thorough knowledge of individual sports through online and offline studies

Postgraduate work covering games as statistician

Developing positive relationships with experienced team statisticians

CAREER PATHS

Some team statisticians freelance as media statisticians

Proven statisticians might join a front office in a player evaluation capacity

RESPONSIBILITIES

Maintain individual and player statistics during games

Serve the front office, including those that work in player evaluation

Provide media with postgame and pregame statistics

In baseball, work as official scorers

Update player and team statistics throughout the season for team and league

MEDIA STATISTICIANS

ACADEMICS

Bachelor's degree, preferably in statistics, mathematics, journalism, or sports analytics

EXPERIENCE

In-game statistician for junior high school, high school, or college teams

Thorough knowledge of individual sports through online and offline studies

Postgraduate work covering games as statistician

Developing positive relationships with sports production companies

CAREER PATHS

Expanding range of sports that can be covered expertly

Possible full-time work as team statistician

RESPONSIBILITIES

Maintain attention in-game on statistics monitor and individual player performance

Detect trends in wide range of player and team statistics

Inform radio or television announcers about findings for dissemination to viewers or listeners

SPORTS ANALYTICS

ACADEMICS

Bachelor's degree, preferably in statistics, sports analytics, or sports management

Beneficial to gain master's degree in statistics, sports analytics, or sports management

EXPERIENCE

Proven analysis of players on home team or opponents at high school or college level

Research and analysis of players that meet the needs of particular professional franchises

Research and analysis of players and teams that are useful to sports media editors

Statistical work with college media

CAREER PATHS

Work with growing number of sports analytics websites such as FanGraphs.com and Baseball Prospectus

Create online analytics site that meets growing need in sports aside from baseball

Join player personnel department of professional sports franchise

Gain promotions within team hierarchy to levels as high as general manager

RESPONSIBILITIES

Evaluate and predict player performance through a wide range of statistical and empirical variables

Maintain thorough knowledge of positive and negative trends in player performance

Keep track of career path of prospects by accurately determining future value

FANTASY SPORTS ANALYST

ACADEMICS

Bachelor's degree, preferably in statistics or journalism

EXPERIENCE

Success as fantasy owner in variety of leagues

Proven fantasy production predictions about athletes

Run a fantasy league and provide player predictions and analysis for owners

Gain and maintain thorough knowledge about player history and performance in variety of sports

CAREER PATHS

Be willing to provide player analysis and predictions without pay online to hone skills and prove accuracy

Launch fantasy website in most knowledgeable sport

Provide résumé and writing samples to websites that pay fantasy analysts

RESPONSIBILITIES

Understand variety of scoring rules in wide range of fantasy leagues

Maintain awareness of strengths and weaknesses of every player in sport of choice.

Predict statistical output in all skills required of every athlete in the sport

Track in-season trends to provide sage advice to owners about trades and lineup choices

BUREAU OF LABOR STATISTICS INFORMATION

Sports statisticians compile and keep track of individual and team statistics for teams, media members, and fans.

About a third of statisticians work for the federal government or for scientific research and development companies. Statisticians work mostly in offices, but such is not the case with sports statisticians, who spend most of their time working at sporting events held in arenas or stadiums.

Those seeking work in player evaluation for professional sports franchises typically need at least a master's degree in statistics, mathematics, or another quantitative field. However, a bachelor's degree is sufficient for other jobs in the sports statistics field.

Employment of statisticians is projected to grow 34 percent over the next several years, much faster than the average for all occupations.

GLOSSARY

analytics The analysis of statistics and other data with the purpose of predicting future player and team performance.

athletic director The head of a high school or college athletic department.

box score A thorough rundown of player and team statistics from one particular game.

data Individual facts, statistics, or items of information.

draft In professional or fantasy sports, the selection of players for the purpose of supplementing or building a roster.

fantasy Activity in a variety of sports in which participants draft and maintain teams of real players whose statistics result in points for the participants.

free agent An athlete who is free to market his or her services to any team.

interview A conversation between an employer and prospective employee in which the former asks questions of the latter to determine if the latter should be hired.

LinkedIn A website on which people in various fields contact each other to promote professional development.

official scorer A person hired by Major League Baseball to track each play in a game and decide if a player deserves an error on a play not completed.

payroll The total amount of employees' salaries within a company or organization.

probability The study of what is most likely to happen based on history or statistical data.

professional An individual who is paid to work and perform a certain job.

résumé A brief written account of past academic and work experience and achievements used to convince employers to hire a prospective employee.

sabermetrics In-depth statistical data used to evaluate and predict player and team performance in baseball.

scouts Professionals who evaluate players through observation and report their findings to the teams for which they work.

social media Various online sites such as Twitter and Facebook that promote interaction between people.

tendencies In sports, likelihood of particular player's or team's performance based on previous outcomes.

Twitter A social media service in which users post short updates or opinions about sports and other subjects.

FOR MORE INFORMATION

American Statistical Association

732 North Washington Street

Alexandria, VA 22314-1943

(888) 231-3473

Website: http://www.amstat.org

The ASA provides a wide range of information for budding statisticians in all fields, including job opportunities and potential salaries. The organization also gives fellowships and grants to promising statisticians.

Association for Women in Sports Media

7742 Spalding Drive

Norcross, GA 30092

Website: http://awsmonline.org

Both men and women can join this organization, which serves to promote the advancement of female students and professionals in sports media.

National Sports Media Association

PO Box 1545

Salisbury, NC 28145

(704) 633-4275

Website: https://nationalsportsmedia.org

The NSMA seeks to develop educational opportunities for those who are interested in pursuing a career in sports media, through networking, interning, mentoring, and scholarship programs.

SAS Institute

100 SAS Campus Drive

Cary, NC 27513-2414

(919) 677-8000

Website: https://www.sas.com/en_us/industry/sports.html

This organization promotes sports analytics and supports prospects and professionals in the field by posting job openings, news, and future events.

Sports Media Canada

44 Hallsport Crescent

Toronto, ON M3M 2K7

Canada

Website: http://www.sportsmediacanada.ca

This organization is part of the International Sports Press Association. It serves as a link between the sports media and sports organizations throughout Canada while promoting meetings and seminars.

Statistical Society of Canada

219-1725 St. Laurent Boulevard

Ottawa, ON K1G 3V4

Canada

(613) 627-3530

Website: https://ssc.ca/en

Among the missions of the SSC are developing public awareness of the value of statistical thinking, promoting a sense of community among all statisticians in Canada, and providing a forum to exchange ideas among statisticians.

WEBSITES

Because of the changing nature of internet links, Rosen Publishing has developed an online list of websites related to the subject of this book. This site is updated regularly. Please use this link to access the list:

http://www.rosenlinks.com/GCSI/Stat

FOR FURTHER READING

Alamar, Benjamin C. *Sports Analytics: A Guide for Coaches, Manager, and Other Decision Makers*. New York, NY: Columbia University Press, 2013.

Crevin, Matt. *Get in the Game: The Ultimate Game Plan for Transition to College to Career*. Voice of the Box Productions, 2012.

Fay, Gail. *Sports: The Ultimate Team Guide*. Lanham, MD: Rowman and Littlefield, 2015.

Freedman, Jeri. *Dream Jobs in Sports Management and Administration*. New York, NY: Rosen Publishing, 2013.

Gitlin, Marty. *Dream Jobs in Sports Scouting*. New York, NY: Rosen Publishing, 2015.

Hahn, Gerald H., and Necip Doganaksoy. *A Career in Statistics: Beyond the Numbers*. Hoboken, NJ: Wiley, 2011.

Harmon, Daniel. *Dream Jobs in Sports Media*. New York, NY: Rosen Publishing, 2014.

Hums, Mary A., and Joanne C. MacLean. *Governance and Policy in Sports Organizations* (Sport Management). London, UK: Routledge, 2013.

McLeish, Ewan. *Sports Industry* (A Closer Look: Global Industries). New York, NY: Rosen Publishing, 2011.

Meltzer, Peter E. *So You Think You Know Baseball: A Fan's Guide to the Official Rules*. New York, NY: W.W. Norton & Company, 2013.

Mooney, Carla. *Cool Careers Without College for People Who Love Sports*. New York, NY: Rosen Publishing, 2017.

Moskowitz, Tobias, and Jon L. Wertheim. *Scorecasting: The Hidden Influences Behind How Sports Are Played and Games Are Won*. Pittsburgh, PA: Three Rivers Press, 2012.

Peters, Elisa, ed. *Statistics and Probability* (The Story of Math). New York, NY: Rosen Publishing, 2015.

Rothman, Stanley. *Learning Statistics with Baseball*. Baltimore, MD: Johns Hopkins University Press, 2012.

Schechter, Larry. *Winning Fantasy Baseball: Secret Strategies of a Nine-Time National Champion*. Emerald Book Company, 2014.

Schultz, Christian Dahl. *Ferguson Career Launcher: Professional Sports Organizations*. New York, NY: Ferguson Publishing, 2011.

Severini, Thomas A. *Analytic Methods in Sports: Using Mathematics and Statistics to Understand Data from Baseball, Football, Basketball, and Other Sports*. London, UK: Chapman and Hall/CRC, 2014.

Shally-Jensen, Michael. *Careers in Sports*. Ipswich, MA: Salem Press, 2017.

Shea, Stephen M., and Christopher E. Baker. *Basketball Analytics: Objective and Efficient Strategies for Understanding How Teams Win*. CreateSpace Independent Publishing Platform, 2013.

Wirkmaa, Andres. *The Complete Baseball Scorekeeping Handbook*. Jefferson, NC: McFarland, 2015.

Wong, Glenn M. *The Comprehensive Guide to Careers in Sports*. Burlington, MA: Jones & Bartlett Learning, 2012.

BIBLIOGRAPHY

Alamar, Benjamin, and Vijay Mehrota. "Beyond 'Moneyball' = Rapidly evolving world of sports analytics, Part 1." *Analytics*. October 2011. http://analytics-magazine.org/beyond-moneyball-the-rapidly-evolving-world-of-sports-analytics-part-i.

Baseball Prospectus. "Fantasy Articles." Retrieved April 2, 2017. http://www.baseballprospectus.com/fantasy.

Bastian, Jordan. "Shapiro shares his thoughts on 'Moneyball.'" *MLB.com*. January 18, 2012. http://m.mlb.com/news/article/26376888.

Battista, Judy. "More N.F.L. teams hire statisticians but their use remains mostly guarded." *New York Times*. November 24, 2012. http://www.nytimes.com/2012/11/25/sports/football/more-nfl-teams-hire-statisticians-but-their-use-remains-mostly-guarded.html.

Baysinger, Tim. "The ACC Finally Lands its Own TV Network Through a Partnership with ESPN." July 21, 2016. http://www.adweek.com/tv-video/acc-finally-lands-its-own-tv-network-through-partnership-espn-172619/.

Bhardwaj, Nirav. "How to get a job in an MLB front office." *Sabergm.com*. Retrieved March 30, 2017. http://www.sabergm.com/job-mlb-front-office/.

Bluey, Rob. "From 'Moneyball' to money bombs: What sports analytics can teach political nerds." *The Atlantic*.

March 8, 2013. https://www.theatlantic.com/politics/archive/2013/03/from-moneyball-to-money-bombs-what-sports-analytics-can-teach-political-nerds/273824.

Bresiger, Gregory. "Nearly 75M people will play fantasy football this year." *New York Post*. September 5, 2015. http://nypost.com/2015/09/05/nearly-75m-people-will-play-fantasy-football-this-year.

Dizikes, Peter. "Six keys to sports analytics." *MIT News*. March 2, 2015. http://news.mit.edu/2015/mit-sloan-sports-analytics-conference-0302.

FanGraphs. Retrieved March 23, 2017. http://www.fangraphs.com.

Fantasy Sports and Mathematics. "Benefits." Retrieved March 17, 2017. http://fantasysportsmath.com/benefits.php.

Fontenot, Albert. "Top 24 Best Sports Management Degree Programs 2014." *Sports Management Degree Guide*. Retrieved March 29, 2017. http://www.sports-management-degrees.com/best-sports-management-degree-programs-2014.

Hamilton, Howard. "Advice to those seeking (sports) analytics careers." *Soccermetrics Research*. December 21, 2015. http://www.soccermetrics.net/misc-stuff/sports-analytics-career-advice.

Hartford Courant. "A timeline of the revolution." Retrieved March 27, 2017. http://articles.courant.com/2004-04-05/sports/0404050117_1_baseball-abstract-stats-balls.

Hruby, Patrick. "The Founding Fathers of Fantasy." Sports on Earth. December 2, 2013. http://www.sportsonearth.com/article/64244480.

Kelly, Jonathan. "Q&A: Fantasy baseball creator Daniel Okrent." *Vanity Fair*. March 2008. http://www.vanityfair.com/news/2008/03/qa-fantasy-base.

Kounang, Nadia. "The time-sucking, dopamine-boosting science of fantasy baseball." *CNN*. March 18, 2016. http://www.cnn.com/2016/03/18/health/fantasy-sports-psychology.

Marshall, John. "Arizona's Chayka becomes youngest GM in NHL history." May 5, 2016. *Associated Press*. http://bigstory.ap.org/article/b28bba8a6e604a8598f66311b7eb79b6/arizonas-chayka-becomes-youngest-gm-nhl-history.

NFL. "Scouting combine." Retrieved March 19, 2017. http://www.nfl.com/combine/workouts.

Pelton, Kevin. "Basic concepts (not math) at the heart of sports analytics." *ESPN.com*. Retrieved March 25, 2017. http://www.espn.com/espn/print?id=17678246&type=Story&images.

Reimer, Alex. "Syracuse University Will Launch First Sports Analytics Degree in the U.S." *Forbes*. May 11, 2016. https://www.forbes.com/sites/alexreimer/2016/05/11/syracuse-university-will-launch-first-sports-analytics-degree-in-the-u-s/#6b9538bd73b4.

Smith, Timothy W. "Pro Football: These days, 4 quarters seem to add up to less." *New York Times*. October 13, 1991. http://www.nytimes.com/1991/10/13/sports/pro-football-these-days-4-quarters-seem-to-add-up-to-less.html.

Stattr@k. "Preparing for a career as a sports statistician: Two interviews with people in the field." August 1, 2012. http://stattrak.amstat.org/2012/08/01/sports-statistician.

Steinberg, Leigh. "Changing the game: The rise of sports analytics." *Forbes*. August 18, 2015. https://www.forbes.com/sites/leighsteinberg/2015/08/18/changing-the-game-the-rise-of-sports-analytics/#698f17ad4c1f.

Stolbunov, Valentin. "Introduction to Sports Analytics." *University of Toronto Sports Analysts Group*. December 11, 2014. http://sportsanalytics.sa.utoronto.ca/2014/12/11/introduction-to-sports-analytics.

Syracuse University. "Sports Analytics, BS." Retrieved March 29, 2017. http://coursecatalog.syr.edu/preview_program.php?catoid=11&poid=6445&returnto=1460.

University of Minnesota. "What Can I Do with a Major in Statistics?" Retrieved March 27, 2017. https://cla.umn.edu/wcidwami/statistics.

Weinberg, Neil. "The Nine Best Baseball Websites." New English D. Retrieved March 24, 2017. https://newenglishd.com/2013/01/12/the-nine-best-baseball-websites.

Winston, Beth. "What kind of math skills does a sports statistician need?" *Houston Chronicle*. Retrieved April 2, 2017. http://work.chron.com/kind-math-skills-sports-statistician-need-3530.html.

INDEX

T

W

Y

ABOUT THE AUTHOR

Marty Gitlin has authored more than one hudnred educational books, many in the world of sports. He won more than forty-five awards as a newspaper sportswriter, including first place for general excellence from Associated Press for his coverage of the 1995 World Series. That organization also selected him as one of the top four feature writers in Ohio in 2001. Gitlin covered the Cleveland Browns for CBSSports.com from 2009 to 2012 before becoming a fantasy football and baseball writer for that website in 2013.

PHOTO CREDITS

Cover, p. 1 (figure) Elena Elisseeva/Shutterstock.com; cover, p. 1 (background) Chad Claeyssen/Shutterstock.com; pp. 4, 68–69, 79, 84 Icon Sportswire /Getty Images; p. 9 Steven Ryan/National Hockey League/Getty Images; pp. 10–11 Bob Leverone/Getty Images; pp. 14–15 Baranq/Shutterstock.com; pp. 18–19 Monkey Business Images/Shutterstock.com; pp. 24–25 gpointstudio /Shutterstock.com; pp. 26–27 Dragon Images/Shutterstock.com; p. 29 Arieliona/iStock/Thinkstock; pp. 32–33, 58–59 © AP Images; pp. 36–37 AF Archive/Alamy Stock Photo; p. 39 Leon Halip/Getty Images; p. 41 Aspen Photo/Shutterstock.com; p. 43 Boston Globe/Getty Images; pp. 46–47 The Washington Post/Getty Images; p. 52 John Lamparski /WireImage/Getty Images; p. 54 Curt Gunther/Sports Illustrated /Getty Images; pp. 60–61 Maykherkevych/Shutterstock.com; pp. 66–67 2p2play/Shutterstock.com; p. 70 RichVintage/E+/Getty Images; p. 74 David Litman/Shutterstock.com; p. 78 Purestock/Thinkstock; p. 81 Andresr/E+/ Getty Images; p. 88 Fort Worth Star-Telegram/Tribune News Service/Getty Images; p. 91 Samo Trebizan/Shutterstock.com; p. 93 Sean M. Haffey/Getty Images; p. 96 New York Times Co./Archive Photos/Getty Images; pp. 100–101 Lipik/Shutterstock.com; interior design elements © www.istockphoto.com/ hudiemm (grid pattern); http://lostandtaken.com (striped border); pp. 8, 22, 35, 51, 64, 77, 90, 103, 106, 112, 113, 115, 118 (montage) © www.iStockphoto.com, Shutterstock.com.

Designer: Brian Garvey; Layout: Ellina Litmanovich;
Editor: Bethany Bryan; Photo Researcher: Sherri Jackson